Teach Me

By Phoenix

Printed in the United States of America

Cover design by Elaina Lee
Edited by Katandra Jackson Nunnally
Final proof by Katandra Jackson Nunnally
& Courtney 'Phoenix' White

First Printing, 2015

ISBN 978-0-9861001-0-9

FreedomInk Publishing
P O Box 1093
Reidsville, Georgia 30453

www.freedomink365.com

1. African American - Erotica
2. Urban Life
3. Erotica - General

Dear Reader,

First off, I would like to wish everyone a happy and prosperous New Year. I would also like to send a shout out to all of my FreedomInk family across the nation, whom are relishing in their continued literary successes. Our Publisher, Katandra Jackson Nunnally, is incomparable. I, Phoenix am writing you on behalf of FreedomInk introducing to you my second novel 'Teach Me'. I am so elated that you all have continued to follow me on this literary journey and I hope that you won't be disappointed with my second debut. I make it my mission to keep you engaged in my thoughts and keep you reading. There is no greater place in the world than your own imagination. I use the genre Erotica to explicitly and subliminally express my thoughts and desires. With each book there is a lesson to learn. Each story has been inspired by many and shatters the myth that others don't understand what you've been through. I may make you wonder, I may make you cry, I may make you crave but just keep reading.

Happy Reading Lovers and for those who are new to these Erotic fantasy tales... Welcome to Phoenix.

Dedication

First and foremost, to women. I love you and your strength to do the dishes, birth the babies, feed the families, do the cleaning, work ungodly shifts, go to school and have time to live out your own aspirations. It's hard and I thank you for being a positive representation of 'Woman'. With all of your accomplishments let me remind you not to be just 'Anybody's Somebody'.
You are your own reward. Own it!

To my publisher, Katandra Jackson Nunnally, I'm convinced you are a super hero. You go to war for your authors. I appreciate your professionalism as well as your welcoming each author as a member of the FreedomInk family. It's FreedomInk against the world! Thank you for believing in me this second time around.

To my sister, Cara, you're always amazing and I'm proud of the young woman you've become. And to my best friends, I wish you all nothing but happiness, good wine, good health and prosperity. I thank you for your patience when I can't always answer the phone but know that I value our friendship to the moon and back.

Shamatee, I told you I would make sure your name was in the dedication. You're the sister everyone believes you are and I thank you very much for your continuous support.

To my parents, I love you and as always, thank you for your support. You believed in me before I did and I think that anyone would agree you did an awesome job!

To Dorian, like my literary journey, I dedicate my love and appreciation to you for sticking by my side and encouraging me to keep striving. We support each other through long nights and even longer days which creates the best results and merit for our artistic efforts.

Forever and ever babe.

Teach Me

By Phoenix

Teach Me

Chapter 1

Mrs. Aminah Goodwin

To be at fault would mean to admit a guilt that I don't think I am ready to own up to. It would have never happened if my heart wasn't broken and I hadn't warranted the option for someone else to make me feel alive again. I often wondered what my life would've been like without either of them, my husband and my lover. I never pegged myself to be unfaithful. A cheater is what I would have accused others to be in the past. Never in a million years could I have imagined my life this way.

As my friends and I approached 40, 10 or so years into marriage, the divorces began, first a trickle, then a torrent. Divorce never had the greatest reputation. Some flee loveless marriages to find themselves after spending close to 20 years catering to everyone's needs but their own or to escape some type of abuse. Some end up in messy legal battles as a result of something minor when they simply should have spent more time repairing their marriage so that they could remain married.

Marriage became an unending chore. Laundry, cooking, and cleaning. In the beginning you are usually distracted by tending to children but I never had any. Every year we talked about the following year having kids and then all of a sudden I was forty and no longer needed in the way I once was. I began to feel irrelevant and inferior to my husband's successful company.

I now understand why the forty-something woman is so vulnerable. There is a window of opportunity, where a compliment can have far more impact than it otherwise would, where attention and fawning over can become as natural to receive as the air we breathe. The grass is rarely greener on that other forbidden side that we sometimes risk everything just for a closer look at the landscape. I have learned that consequences are often fueled by the inconvenience of Karma and conscience and that a good marriage requires work. It is a test of endurance that is filled with joys, and laughter, tears, and worries, and sometimes pain. If you stick with it, the joys will always outweigh the pain. Sometimes marriage is boring. Sometimes marriage is exciting and changes with the season. Sometimes it stays the same. As for that younger man who makes you feel like they have the ability to physically pump the blood into your veins again, he is rarely the soulmate you tell yourself he is.

I empathized with my friends when they complained that there were no decent guys out there. Consoled them when dating led to being dumped. And provided companionship when they were their most lonely and their children could not fill the void. They said I was lucky. And honestly, I was at some point. Early on, marriage was a good time for me. It was time for me to grow and expand my horizons. I had a lot to be grateful for, I realized. I also learned through observation and experience where I went wrong. I loved my husband and I know he loved me. But after 10 years I knew that I wasn't emotionally or sexually satisfied. I became jealous of my newly single friends partaking in raunchy sexual ventures from the inside of their own cars to sneaking around in restaurant bathrooms. It was through them that I discovered the joys of having sex but I couldn't imagine having sex with someone I was lusting after instead of someone that was within my own home. Well, when he was there.

I had never had an orgasm by any man before my lover which includes my husband. It's not that the sex between my husband and I wasn't good, he just didn't press the right buttons. Don't get me wrong I enjoyed sex with my husband. He was amazing in bed. If he wasn't away so much, I would have never opened Pandora's Box. My lover made me laugh in a way my husband hadn't in so long. I know its cliché and horrible of me to assume that a few giggles is what provoked me to spread my legs. I was empty and sought fulfillment much to my own chagrin. Suddenly, I want to get away from him, my husband. It happened that quickly. Yes, my husband has suspicions of my ever changing moods, but it was my decision to continue to deceive him. I became very self-absorbed. Maybe it's just my guilty heart. And although I broke the sanctity of our vows by laying with another man, there wasn't a moment that passed that I wasn't craving my husband and the familiarity of his body.

I could hear my attorney's heels interrupting my thoughts as they click clacked down the linoleum hallway. Hmm, Christian Louboutin's, I thought as I shifted positions in that uncomfortable steel chair. In walks this attractive young tender piece. Bright complexion, wearing a black on black pant suit. Not a hair out of place, no makeup and nice full lips. Pouty like mine. But I imagine her to live a boring life. All this legal mumbo jumbo and no snap, crackle, and pop! I wonder when was the last time she had a freaking orgasm... Or even if she's ever had one. Oh my God, she's never had an orgasm! I'm sure of it. That's the reason behind this plain Jane black and white fixture of flesh. I processed all of these thoughts within the thirty or so seconds it took her to take her seat in front of me.

"Mrs. Aminah Goodwin, we meet again."

"Indeed we do Ms. Reynolds."

Attorney Mai Reynolds is a bad ass attorney, I must say. I had to get the best. And after countless consultations I found her. To clear my name. To salvage what is left of my now tarnished reputation. To remove the stained Scarlett A from my chest. I have great faith in her desire to help me.

"Before I break this down for you Ms. Reynolds..."

"Please call me Mai."

"Mai... The first thing I am paying you for is not to judge me. I don't have any friends. They are long gone. As for the indiscretion, I'm not quite sure if I can blame it on the devil or boredom but it happened. I could've stopped it at any point in time but I kept going back. He was poison. He, Micah, my lover... Well, former lover, was everything I thought I wanted in a man. He was everything I needed at the time. Companionship is important to me. Laughter and raunchy sex trumped its #1 spot. A whole world of Hell is my reward for giving in to such temptation. Even now, I think about the way his body harmonized with the rhythms of my own and the way his tongue used to dance... And it did dance. I miss it. I should have known better. I knew better. However, I've tasted and I have been satisfied. That is something that cannot be forgotten or undone. This ain't no Mary Kay Letourneau type of shit. Me and Micah obviously cannot get married, but he was well of age when we began our affair."

"So you admit that you did in fact have an affair with Micah Ford?" She said as she scribbled something seemingly of importance in her notebook.

"Let me ask you this. Should we define it as an affair when my husband was completely absent Mai?"

"Aminah, listen, you're an educated woman, you made a mistake a lot of women make while they are married. Experts say a lonely wife may be susceptible to the advancements of another man. And over 50% of married women cheat on their husbands. The bottom line here is that you were LEGALLY married, absent husband or not."

"Mai, we are not just talking about a few advancements that may have influenced your 'experts' theory. We are talking about pure unadulterated, steamy, toe-tingling, lip biting, fucking. On the regular. It wasn't equivalent to the same boring meal every day. Spaghetti, chicken, hamburgers. Micah was that lobster tail and truffle butter followed by the most decadent of desserts. That man was a flavor creator. He was unequivocally mind-racing. He touched my palette in a way my husband had never."

"Your husband did find out about the affair did he not?"

"Yes."

"And what was his reaction?"

"Are you married?" I asked while avoiding her previous question.

"Yes." Mai replied.

"Have you ever had the type of sex with your husband that made your temple and brow sweat just by recollection?" Mai shifted her weight from one side to the other.

"Micah made me do and feel things I had never felt before. "

By just speaking of sex with Micah, Mai's eyes grew in size and her tense frame began to relax itself into her chair. She wants to know more. She ain't never had what I had so how could she ever gather the ultimate truth. Or maybe she has.

Let me start from the beginning...

The Beginning of the End of Me

How could this be? The beginning and the end?

Admission of sin and a marriage that may never mend

I cannot hide anymore and I will not bend

No alibi to take the guilt, no next of kin

I take responsibility for the mess that I'm in

Though the lust in my eyes

should have come as no surprise

But I deserve to be reprimanded for all those lies

For a man I thought deserved the prize between my thighs

I am done borrowing loyalty's disguise

My existence is tarnished in exchange for time to stand still

Desiring for you to understand

the madness beneath my ink quill

I do not mean for my mistakes to become a trend

Because once it starts, it is the beginning of the end.

Chapter 2

Imperfect or Unmatched

I'll be honest. I'm probably the most put together of my two best friends Celeste and Laurisse. I married the love of my life, I have a good job at Kensington College teaching a course entitled Great Books I. Sean and I don't have any children of our own yet but we plan to. Well, I plan to run it past him soon. He's so busy all the time we hadn't had a moment to just sit and talk about any future arrangements. I was pregnant once but I miscarried. We were just married and barely ready to provide for a little one. Sean made it his mission to get our finances in order to try again. That was ten years ago. I'm almost the big 4-0 however my grandmother had her last child at 42 and the doctor says I am in great health and shape to bear at least one child before it is too late.

My friend Celeste has one daughter, Larae, whom I adore. I adore all of my God kids the same. The other two are Laurisse's children. Celeste is an Accountant who steals the hearts of many men but is never satisfied. She invests herself into far too many people. If they don't measure up to her portrait of success she drops them and moves on. The only thing that has sustained in her life over the past ten years is her career. She enjoys being an Accountant, however she has trouble maintaining her own finances. It is so bad that if we go out to eat I often catch her stealing tips from waited tables on her premeditated trip to the restroom before we depart from the restaurant and head home. I don't bring it up. If she gets caught then it's on her. I do not need her acts of desperation leaking onto my reputation. I do however try to help her out whenever possible. At least until she marries rich which I assume is what she is aspiring to accomplish. She is very supportive of my husband and I and our marriage. It could be that she admires the financial stability more than anything but nevertheless, she always seemed very fond of my husband Sean since the first introduction.

I love everything about my husband. He's successful, he's funny, he's charming, and very sexy. His kissable clean shaven pecan complexion is one of his many complimenting features. He's my best friend. I married my best friend. He would do absolutely anything for me as I for him.

I opened the windows in our plush bedroom and inhaled the new day. It was an absolute gorgeous day which was peculiar for September in Seattle. It smelled like summer sunshine instead of rain and it was warmer than usual.

"Morning baby." I said as I ran my hand over Sean's chest.

"G'Mornin sweetheart." he replied as he rolled over to meet my face. He kissed me sweetly on the forehead and got up quickly to put his robe on and go over to his desk in our room to login to his work email.

"Babe, ya wanna pee first before you dive right in to work?" Guess I'm lucky I at least got a smooch out of the deal huh?

"Fret not my beautiful curvaceous wife," he said with a fake English accent. "I'm getting ready to close on a very large development deal in the Hampton's. I'm just anxious to get the nod from the big wigs and then I need to book my flight." he stated with pride and no eye contact.

Disappointed. "You're leaving again?"

"Baby this is huge for us. More money, more opportunities for us love. I'm not leaving immediately honey, I should still be here until after your birthday next month. I will be here to celebrate with my smart, sexy, ever supportive dear, dear wife, that I am about to make mad passionate love to." he stated matter-of-factly as he turned around and crawled up the end of the bed and pulled me close to him.

After about 3 and a half minutes of four play and 7 minutes of gentle thrusting, he was satisfied. I had to laugh to myself. That's my husband. Sex wasn't always so scarce. When his company was solely stationed here he used to call off from work just so he could hit it all day. I guess the thrill of it all is over. Sex has become routine. I'm 39 and a childless old married woman. Who knew this would be the result of a successful black couple in Seattle. Sometimes I think the rain is more stimulating than my love life. At least it's consistent. If it comes down between my husband's thriving and successful architectural business and me, the business wins every time.

Guess me and the peace sign have a hot date tonight while mister is working, I thought to myself as I headed downstairs to whip up some breakfast for my brown suga who is left typing his way into carpal tunnel in our bedroom.

Repetition must have been my middle name in a past life because currently my world clearly lacks variety. After getting dressed in my black on black pant suit and a quick kiss on the cheek so as to not mess up my primped M.A.C. beat face, I drove myself to the only place I find a little bit of variation. Work. It was September 1st, class was back in session for the new semester. There would be a new syllabus and a new class, but the same daily grind.

I walked into class confident and ready to teach. 23 students registered for the course which meant between 15-18 students will actually show up and maybe 12-15 will stay for the entire course. I don't take it personal. I was a student once. Schedules change, major's change, shit happens. After roll call, 17 students showed up for the first day. I was impressed.

"Hello class, my name is Dr. Aminah Goodwin and you will primarily find me here in Carroll Hall at Kensington College. I hope that this semester is pleasantly challenging for you. This class is offered on Monday's, Wednesdays, and Friday's from 5:30 to 6:45. If you ever need assistance, my phone number and email address are both on the syllabus for your access for any questions or concerns to increase success in the course. You may contact me any time day or night and I will respond as quickly as possible. I want to get to know you all.

Getting to know you will enable me to personalize a learning plan for the class overall. Each class is different because each student is different. My aim is to accommodate each one of you as long as you give me your best effort in return."

"Well then I'll be giving you all the effort you need Dr. G.", exclaimed Micah Ford, a senior taking my course.

There were a few giggles that erupted from his peers.

"Thank you Mr. Ford," I said intending not to expound upon his remarks to urge him on. "So let's get started. The Great Books I syllabus is applicable to both Great Books I and Great Books II courses. The headings and topics covered below are in red.

"Sexy" Micah murmured.

"Excuse me?" I said as I lowered my glasses to see who was speaking out of context presumably thinking it was Micah Ford again.

"No. Excuse me." Micah said sarcastically.

"Uhh. Um... Anyhow the schedule and reading list is at the bottom of this syllabus. All students are required to read the weekly assigned reading including at least one poem as a prerequisite for participation in the weekly seminar discussion. And now for the meat and potatoes of the course which is indeed my favorite part... The Books! Ladies and gentlemen this is not a course in ancient writings such as Plato and The Odyssey, which don't get me wrong, they are classics. Let's just say we'll be studying just a few years beyond those folks." I said sarcastically.

"Samiya Bashir, Margaret Walker, Ed Roberson, Walter de la Mare, are to name a few of whom we may delve into. I wish I could fit every great author and poet into one semester, and there is always someone I don't want to leave out but have to. Then there are those that I remember after the semester is over and I will be at home in the middle of some daunting chore and it will dawn on me and out of nowhere my husband will hear me profess out loud "Ooo! I should have talked about such and such." I'm sure he thinks I'm crazy when I begin conversations with myself about work but he loves me enough to keep me around."

I passionately spoke about the books and required readings expected of my students this semester for almost a solid hour. After every sentence, I would catch Micah's eye. The other students were texting in their phones or typing away on their laptops what I hoped to be notes from my lecture. Micah on the other hand was listening intently. I don't believe he picked up his pen once except to twirl the cap around in his mouth. I think that if I gave a pop quiz on everything covered today, not only would Micah be the only 100% A, but he would write what I said verbatim. I hate when people stare at me like that. It makes me feel insecure or that I'm uninteresting and their minds have drifted off elsewhere. My husband does this. Sometimes it's like talking to a brick wall.

"Well, after talking everyone's ear off today you are free to go, I promise things will be more interactive and less lecture on Wednesday. Good luck everyone and I wish you all an amazing semester."

I took a seat at my desk and sipped my now lukewarm green tea. My teaching tenure stretches more than ten years and yet the first day still makes my knees buckle from nervousness.

"Hey Dr. G." Startled. I looked up and it was the same obnoxious guy from earlier, Micah Ford.

"Yes Micah?"

"I just wanted to let you know I enjoyed your lecture today."

"Well thank you Micah, I can appreciate that."

"No problem. Enjoy your evening."

"Thanks, you too." I was forced to retract my previous thoughts. Maybe he wasn't as obnoxious as I had assumed. I smiled to myself. He had a little southern drawl. Cute. I wonder where he's from originally.

Guess I should grab some dinner on the way home. I do not feel like cooking after running my mouth for an hour and 15 minutes. I just need food to replace all that energy and my pillows to welcome me with heavenly comfort. As I glance over the room, it is clean except for one lonely piece of paper lying face down on one of the desks. I turned it over and it read:

<u>Undivided Attention</u>
Paying attention to you like a well-trained
Pit Bull to your every move
I'd like for us to put on a record and groove
I feel compelled to tell you how beautiful you are
Bet you think I can't tell from afar
Eyes of chestnut brown and skin fresh like morning dew
The most perfect mural anyone ever drew
I'd like to begin an evening pleasing... You
I'd begin by kissing up to the knee
This is pleasant you might agree
As I finally reach your smiling face

Our lips join with close embrace

I'd take extra good care of you,

I've observed that you are special

Nights would welcome the sweetest slumber

when you lay on my chest and nestle

For I've looked in your eyes today and we connected

Any pain you have been feeling I've now intercepted

I know you think I was obnoxious every time I interjected

But I needed your full attention

for it's the lion in me you have erected

I admire your love for poetry

so I will rhythmically alleviate any tension

My apologies for the outbursts, just know I was paying

attention...

Chapter 3

Vault

"Oh my damn!" Laurisse said while snapping and popping her Big Red gum in response to me reading the letter left after my lecture. I called an emergency meeting with my girls at the Winery and Dessert Bar. Though educated I could not make heads or tails of this dilemma on my own.

"I know right!" I said.

"So you think it was the guy that was making all those comments during class?" Celeste asked while devouring her strawberry cheesecake.

"I don't know for sure. It was a pretty mixed class however Micah would be too obvious of a match. I don't want to assume. Ya know?"

"Oh fuck that, you need to assume and accuse! That man wants to sample your snack box chick. Haha!"

"Shut up Celeste... Really?"

"REALLY! Haha. I mean seriously read between the lines, hell you are the poetry buff! If not him then who?!" She beamed.

"I guess you're right Celeste but how do I handle this? Do I just let it go? It's not like he left it on my desk and signed his name to it so I can't report it to anyone without hardcore evidence."

"Girl you watch too much Law and Order. I say call his ass out on it and see what he says and then address it accordingly." Laurisse chimed in.

"That's the thing. How do I 'address' it? Do I walk up and say, Hey Micah I found this face down on your desk yesterday, I'm reprimanding you for saying I was beautiful? That is absurd." I admitted.

"It goes beyond him complimenting your looks Aminah. He wants you girl. You betta be careful." Laurisse said. "I know you didn't speak of anything in regards to kissing ya all over and beyond and shit in your lecture."

I giggled. "No, I did not."

"You have nothing to worry about Aminah, you love Sean. Y'all are good right?"

I dropped my head. When I lifted it back up there were a pair of hazel and a pair of dark brown eyes peering into my soul.

"Uh oh…" Celeste said. "Trouble in paradise?"

"No, we are fine. I just wish he were home more and any way that has nothing to do with this letter."

"Well, distance will kill a relationship. I thought he was home all last week? Did you get to spend time with him then?"

"You could say that. Physically he was in my presence. There was a lot of double dating. Me, him, his phone and his laptop. Shit, I'll take him ignoring me to watch a football game. That is only a couple hours out of the day. But from sun up to sun down to sometimes sun up again, his attention is affixed to the screens and I submit myself to excessive dieting to maintain my figure and porn to maintain my sexual appetite. Pathetic if you ask me. I mean, we've only been married for ten years. You'd think we were about to celebrate our 50th wedding anniversary."

"Chile if you're masturbating 50 years from now, I applaud you." Celeste said clapping.

"Haha, I probably will be if he keeps this up."

"Well what does he say? How does he feel about his actions? How does he feel about another man writing you these fuck invitations?"

"These are not 'fuck invitations' Laurisse. I thought it was beautiful."

"Aw shit. He wants to fuck you girl. And good too."

"Ladies we must keep this a secret. Vault?"

"Vault." They chimed in tune.

"Okay, well, thank you for listening and the zero advice I received on this matter. Haha. I gotta go, I have had a long and eventful day."

"I bet you Micah would like to be your homework!" Laurisse cackled.

"Mmmhmm. Indeed!" Celeste nodded in agreement.

"Goodbye tramps."

"Bye Dr. Freak Nasty." Laurisse bellowed from afar as I was walking out the door. A couple in passing just stared at me as I walked down the steps towards my Lexus.

As I sat and put the key into the ignition, my right thigh vibrated. I pulled my phone out of my pocket and noticed it was my student, Vanessa Norris. After answering her concerns about the Skills Assessment Essay I assigned, my phone vibrated again. I assumed it was Vanessa. That girl is always disputing something or questioning something else. Gal needs a hobby. I glanced over my cell phone once more this time it was not Vanessa and it was a number I did not have plugged in yet. The message read: "Dr. G., I was wondering I can get your insight on how I've supported my thesis for this week's essay?"

I responded with speedy fingers, "Hello this is Dr. Goodwin, may I ask which student I am corresponding with." I quickly responded "I want more than just the facts. Your grade will be determined by how well you demonstrate your knowledge of the facts and your understanding of those facts in a greater context. In terms of supporting, I want you to exhibit that you know how to analyze what your chosen author is saying through poetry."

The reply: "This is Micah Ford. And thank you."

A sudden rush went to my head and my knees buckled. I responded, "Thank you for your questions Micah and have a great evening." I had to keep it professional. Although I must confess, he is attractive and I am indeed flattered. Oh what is wrong with me? Do I lack attention that bad that I could possibly enjoy the affection of another man? A student for God's sake Aminah, I scolded myself. Maybe I just need a male friend. I'm thinking gay so as to not upset my husband. Yes. That's what I need. A gay male best friend. That compliments me like Micah...

Escape

I need him to make me feel like I have a reason for being

My husband and I may be doomed as far as I'm seeing

But I'll give him my best and every effort

I don't need a man in training, I need an expert

I want him to disrupt this dreadful non complacency

I want to see some emotion in his face

while he's sexing me

I have an insatiable appetite that needs to be satisfied

I need more than a slow ride and a smack on the ass

I want him to initiate cunnilingus

while we're flying first class

Bobbin in your lap, no weave... In

This is strength and condition... Just leave... In

I want to touch you and you grow as much as I desire

Surely there is nothing that could extinguish this fire

Confidence grows on my face

as you meet my prerequisite

Laced with your potency held in place by two thick

thighs to preface it

I'll show you what I imagined... This

Chin facing the ceiling making my thighs clap rhythms

anyone's ever rhymed over

Wishful thinking, four leaf clover

I don't want to like the attention of any other man
But curiosity is more than I can stand
I find myself submissive to the hero syndrome I need to
look beyond the cape
But my powers have been weakened by the fantasy of
this sweet escape

Chapter 4

Happy Birthday To Me

It's been three weeks since I've seen my husband and at least three days since the last phone call. I woke up for my birthday anxious for my Sean to come home. Shower, make-up, dress and wait for my husband. That is the plan, I thought as I rolled out of the covers. He wished me happy birthday at midnight just as he always does every year when he is away via text message which I feel is so impersonal but I did not complain. Call me passive. I just want him here. I'm looking forward to him coming through the doors with a big bouquet of flowers. Tulips, lilies, or maybe orchids. Hell, I'll take a handful of wilted fucking dandelions at this point. A funeral shouldn't be the only time a woman receives flowers, I thought to myself picking out one of my mother's clever southern theories to repeat out loud. After applying the blush to my cheeks as a finishing touch to my face and unrolled my hair, I felt presentable enough to greet my king.

I grabbed my phone to respond to some well birthday wishes when Sean's picture graced my phone screen as he was calling. I answered anticipating disappointment.

"Hey Babe!" I said while trying to shake off my negative thinking.

"Baby, I'm sorry I'm not going to make it home in time for your birthday."

"Sean, you promised you would be here."

"I know Aminah, I'm sorry. I go to the board tomorrow to present a new deal. I misunderstood the time for it. By the time the meeting ends and I catch a flight back to Seattle it will be over and you will probably be on your way to bed." 'It' referring to a milestone birthday he promised to be in attendance for. I cried.

"You can't just come home tonight for cake? At least?!" I pleaded in tears.

"Baby don't cry. Don't cry, I'll be there this weekend. I'll have something planned for us both okay? I promise."

"You promise?" I scoffed. "Your promises do nothing but break my heart and your 'almosts' don't count anymore Sean. Goodbye."

"Aminah I don't have time for this."

"You obviously don't have time for anything. You don't have time to have cake with your wife, you don't have time to hug me, or kiss me, and even our fucking is on calculated time!! I'm beginning to wonder how you make time to wipe your ass after you shit!" I hurled at him.

"Not this again Aminah."

"Oh yes Sean, its 'this' again."

"When are you going to let me work to take care of you and not have to worry about your temper tantrums?"

"When you stop worrying about a pay check and be concerned about the wife you leave every couple days."

"What do I have to be concerned about Aminah? We took vows and I know you're safe."

"If that's all you believe are concerns then we are in more trouble than me just wanting you to be intimate with me."

He paused silently and what seemed like an hour was only a minute. "I love you Minah. I'll see you soon and I hope enjoyment finds you for your birthday. See you soon baby."

I hung up without uttering another word. Alone again. I'm 40. It's bittersweet. I love growing in preparation for the next decade. I'm aging well. I have no regrets on my life. If I died when the clock strikes 12 I would be content. Except... Maybe one good fuck before I meet my maker. I'd opt to go out in style. I'd prefer to be ascended on something thick that delivers the elated sensation of transcending into immortality.

Wishful thinking. As wishful as receiving a salivating tongue in between my legs on top of my birthday cake. I heard that women over 40 have a higher libido. They aren't kidding. To make things crystal clear, I'd rather have my back blown out instead of wasting valuable time blowing out 40 fucking candles. But I digress.

I have to get something to eat so I guess I will treat myself. Table for one indeed. I'd rather be by myself as opposed to inviting my friends out to vent about my marriage. They'll do nothing but chastise me for being so mean to Sean and then begin talking about their own lives seeking advice. I don't know which is worse, coming to them for some support and end up giving them advice or sitting across from Sean as he is glued to his phone or tablet, whichever guest he decides to bring to dinner. I'd rather pay my own damn self a few hours of attention. At least I can hold a conversation.

I rolled down the windows in my Lexus and let the awkwardly warm breeze brush the hair away from my face and dry the tears that I repeatedly had to dab with tissue. I freshened up my makeup and pulled near the curb to meet Valet at The Ocean View Restaurant and Hotel. I handed the driver my keys and started in to be seated by the Maître D. After finding a table that was satisfactory and within cozy low lighting and distanced from all the commotion from the front desk I sat and began to stuff my cheeks with the carb-filled, complimentary bread at my table. I must look pretty pathetic sitting here by myself but I don't care. I need to keep my mind off of Micah and my husband is of course out of town. The waitress keeps coming back to my table and calling me "Honey" and "Sweetie" seemingly extra with the niceties and offering me dessert items. I just want to enjoy my seafood and bread in peace. I wish she would knock it off.

I'm alone but not desperate although I can't help but stare at neighboring couple as they share sweet kisses across the table. The baby girl between them is giggling and flailing about. It's about 9:00pm, why do they have her out so late? It's chilly out and certainly too late for that sweet lil one to be awake. I'm not a parent but I am a Godparent to three. I do know a few things. As she bangs her bottle on the table for attention giggling all the while, I just smiled. I have just enough time left to have a baby if I wanted to. But I guess I would need to have sex to do that. My significant other has to be home in order to have sex so I guess I am 0 for 2. Shit. I thought that success and money would have made our lives so easy. Financially yes, but I do want a family of 3 or more. If nothing else, I just want my fucking husband again. I want him to be home. I am starting to feel like I am without purpose. He doesn't compliment me anymore. We don't share meals anymore. The problem is not just this but that he seems content with it being this way.

My somewhat taunting thoughts started to become clouded by thoughts of Micah. *Why do we have so much in common? He's a frickin kid!* I began scolding myself. Erykah Badu's 'Next Lifetime' began playing in my head. I feel like whenever we meet again in the next life, we will be the same age and equally single. Why is he so charming?

"Hmmph! Charming mutha fucka!" I said out loud as I sipped my Sauvignon Blanc and tore apart the King Crab legs I ordered.

"You should really switch to red, it's healthier for you." I looked up suddenly and almost dropped my glass. For a moment I thought I was still daydreaming. There he stood plain as day, as handsome and as charismatic as he possibly could.

"Hi...Mm-Micah, how are you? What are you doing here?" I stammered.

"Umm, I'm hungry... Service is fast and the food is great here although I am concerned that they call it 'Ocean View' and this is Seattle, he said laughing as he sat down, opened his cloth napkin and laid it across his lap.

Damn... I want him to put me across his lap. I want him to bend me over this table and put me smooth out of this depression and vulnerability over... And over... And o--

"Dr. G?"

"Huh?"

"I said actually I work here and just got off. I saw you sitting. Were you expecting someone?" he asked as he looked around.

"Uh, no... I was actually finishing up." (Lying)

"Hmm okay but you haven't had dessert..."

(My thoughts) *Baby I am your dessert...*

"Umm, Micah, I'm not so sure that this is appropriate. I am still your Instructor."

"Well Dr. G... I need you to 'instruct' and 'advise' me on how to maintain my boyish figure and continue to work here with all of this wonderful seafood available to partake in at a discount," he said while signaling for a waiter to come over.

"Hey Brandon, can you get us another bottle of Sauvignon Blanc and two slices of Cinna-Sin Cheesecake. Put a candle in hers." he gestured towards me. "It's her birthday."

"How did you know that?" I asked.

"You mentioned it on the first day of class and you also welcomed any and all gifts off site I do recall. So enjoy. Anything you want is on me. Don't worry, it'll be our secret. This place exceeds any college kids' budget, and it's late so you won't see any."

"Okay." Aw shit what am I saying? Okay? That's all Minah?

No rebuttal, not one?!

"Glad you see it my way Dr. G.'

"Well Micah, if we are to be informal you cannot call me Dr. G., you may call me—"

"Aminah." He said smiling.

"Aminah. Yes. Thank you."

"Tell me about you Micah," I asked in hopes to squeeze out his admission to the poem. "You seem so serious all the time. What are you trying to hide Micah?"

"What are you trying to show me, Aminah?"

I gulped pretty hard and obvious.

He continued. "Well, I'm from Texas. I'm a little late going to college and finishing. My parents couldn't afford to send me when everyone else began at 17 and 18 years old so I started at 21 after excessive scholarship researches and awarding and community assistance. Your class was an upper level elective and the last one I needed so here I am."

"Nice. I'm glad you didn't give up on your dreams. Do your parents still live in Texas?"

"My mom does. Dad died. Heart attack."

"Oh, I'm so sorry."

"It's okay. So tell me about you, besides what was on the syllabus. Do you have any aspirations? Any regrets?"

"No regrets yet that I know of and I aspire to be a great literary genius. I would like to publish a Pulitzer Prize piece of literature and take convincing serious photos like this," as I posed and flashed an award winning smile.

"You have an amazing smile if I may compliment."

"Thank you." I said blushing.

"So you're married." He said as he assumed by the ring I was wearing. "Where is he tonight?"

"He's residing in noneofyourbusinessville."

"Haha, okay, okay. I was just curious as to why you're here alone."

"I wish you would ask this many questions in class Micah instead of daydreaming."

"I can't help myself. If you knew what I was daydreaming about, you would do the same."

"Hmm." I said as I bit my lip. "What about you? Where's your girlfriend? She must be awfully lonely tonight while you're cozying up to some old broad."

"Oh please you are not old, just older than me. If I had a girlfriend she would not be much younger than you."

"I see."

"Here ya go Meek." Brandon served the cheesecake and the wine, smiled at us and slowly walked away while giving Micah a thumbs up.

"See! I need to go."

"Come on Aminah, he doesn't know anything. He just saw a beautiful woman out with a man having cheesecake. He's not going to go running to the Dean to report you."

I settled myself and stared at Micah intently. He has the most beautiful eyes I thought to myself. Absolutely enchanting. And this accent and the chivalry he displays compliments him even more. As he lit the candle on my cheesecake he sat next to me and squeezed my thigh. I admit, I flinched a little.

"Make a wish." He said.

I closed my eyes just barely, hoping that this wasn't a joke and the entire Kensington staff wasn't going to come out and smash the cake on my face on live television. Laurisse and Celeste were right. I do watch too much tv. When I opened my eyes, Micah was staring at me. He moved back to the seat across from me.

"So what are you doing after this?" He asked.

"I think you're too young for me to answer that question." I laughed. "I am actually going upstairs and turning in. It's my birthday and I can sleep if I want to."

"Let me guess, you have a husband that's working hard or hardly working out of town."

"Working. Bingo."

"Do you want the rest of the bottle? I'll have Brandon cork it and send it up."

"Sure why not."

"Great." He motioned once more for Brandon to come back.

"How old are you Micah?" I inquired.

"25."

"25?!"

His eyebrows furrowed. "What's wrong with that?"

"I just didn't expect you to be that young. You're so…"

"Charming?" He said as he adjusted his tie.

"Yes. That and confident. You have an old soul. I never would have pegged you for 25."

"Well I am all of that. Had to be. My parents never had much so I had to grow up quick. It's a gift and a curse."

"How so?"

"Well, it's a gift because I know more than the average. It's a curse because I am underestimated by the most beautiful women because of a number."

"I'm sorry if I've offended you."

"It's okay Aminah. I'm used to it. No worries."

As he helped Brandon box up the remainder of my cheesecake and put my bottle of wine in a wine bag, he pulled out my chair and began to walk me towards the elevator.

"Hey why don't you come to this party with me? The night is still young."

"And so are you Micah. I should be getting off to bed. I'm not really in the mood for any more partying. And plus, didn't I assign you homework you should be working on?"

Girl you are his homework is all I kept hearing Laurisse say in my head.

"It's close, we wouldn't have to walk very far. It's just down a couple blocks."

"I guess I could use a real drink", I said trusting his instincts. "But there is a storm coming and I forgot my umbrella at home." I debated.

Micah scanned the entrance. "I'll be right back." He disappeared behind the hotel desk which was no longer busy and into a room. When he reappeared he was carrying a large black umbrella. "Don't worry it's the hotel's. We'll return it when we come back."

"Oh my. Well, I guess... Let's go."

"Ma'am," Micah said as he extended his arm to escort me.

"Oh God do me a favor and never call me 'Ma'am' "I cringed. "I just turned 40 and I won't have any of that crazy talk."

"Haha, will do Aminah."

The DJ blared some God awful rap that Micah knew I was not feeling from the moment we stepped foot into Club Euphoria.

"Come on." He said as he reached for my hand.

It was then I started to shamefully feel butterflies and any ounce of respect I had for my husband was fading away fast. I took his hand and followed his lead. Just that small embrace eased my heart and my thoughts. There was a stairwell illuminated by red light coming from the basement. When we reached the bottom of the steps, we entered the scarlet room and a low grumbling of combined conversation and laughter. There were very few places to sit down. The velvet crush sofas were occupied by couples and the bar stools were warmed by the asses of single women in skin tight 'come hither' dresses and legs that that invited any eligible bachelor. The music was light and offered the best renditions of R&B of the 90's I have ever heard. As Pretty Brown Eyes by Mint Condition began to sound, I became entranced.

"Oooo! That is my song!" Micah admired me as I began singing along and snapping my fingers.

"Do you want to dance? He asked.

"No one else is dancing." I said as I looked around.

"I bet you 2 shots they will start dancing as soon as we do." He said.

"Bet." I said as I got up. I guess I really wanted to dance. I would have been a little more apprehensive any other time. But it's my birthday. I needed this more than I realized. No more words were exchanged as Micah grabbed me by my hips and wrapped his hands around my waist and we began to sway back and forth. He never took his gaze off of me. I leaned in and closed my eyes, inhaling long and soft. I peered up at the ceiling and felt like I was in a dream. I looked around the floor and all of the couples that were on the sofas were now following our lead. I whispered in Micah's ear, "Guess I owe you two shots."

"Don't worry about it, I just wanted you to be near me for more than an instant. I'm savoring the moment because I may not ever get it back."

Desperately trying to ignore the romantic vibes running through my veins I leaned back and as I did, the storm outside knocked out the electricity.

I heard a few gasps, scrambles from other patrons and a shriek coming from one of the female bartenders. While the lights were out I felt Micah pull me close to him to keep me safe. God he smelled delicious. I could feast on this man all night. He wrapped his arms around me and I turned to face him and felt for the back of his neck and then cheek. I kissed it sweetly and as friend zoned as I could. He lowered his head.

I could feel his sweet breath against my lips. He then leaned back as if to stop himself from kissing me. He made me wrap my arms around his waist and follow him. He led the way into the pitch blackness. I didn't know where we were going but I trusted him. He then pressed me up against the wall. I felt him lean in again. It was slow. Intimate. Passionate. I felt his breath against my lips once more. It was mind blowing and toe tingling. Pussy dripping. It was like eating dessert, naked, in a Jacuzzi, by the fireplace. You may even have to add an ecstasy pill to that equation. SHIT! This is all I wanted. This feeling. Speaking but not exchanging a single word. Touching but feeling like I'm floating on air. Euphoria indeed.

The lights came back on and everyone quickly walked up the stairs to exit the club. It was still raining and even though Micah tried desperately to shield me with the oversized umbrella, we were both soaked. I wouldn't be caught dead without makeup anywhere but this time it is by default. My face was washed clean.

"I hope your night hasn't been ruined by the rain and that I made your birthday somewhat eventful since your husband is away." Micah said as we entered through the brass doors of The Ocean View.

"Poor guy. Doesn't know how good he has it at home."

God, say something Aminah. Defend your husband! Say Goodnight and goodbye. You can't just remain speechless! I thought to myself.

"Thank you for a good time Micah. I really enjoyed myself." I said as I pulled my hair up in a chignon bun.

"You deserved it. Wow, you're so beautiful even after the rain."

"Thanks." I said blushing.

"Oh your food and wine, let me go grab it." Micah said as he turned to return the umbrella we borrowed and walked towards the kitchen where he left the cheesecake and wine.

Honestly in the split second he was gone, I missed him in my presence. He returned with my bag in hand and initiated a hug goodbye.

"When I lie where shades of darkness. Shall no more assail mine eyes. Nor the rain make lamentation. When the wind sighs. How will fare the world whose wonder, was the very proof of me? Memory fades, must the remembered. Perishing be? See you in class Dr. G. Goodnight." Micah said as he tapped my chin smiling and walked away.

"Hey that's Walter de la Mare's Farewell! Someone's been reading! Goodnight."

I went to my room, kicked off my stilettos and lay down in my soft hotel bed. Unaccompanied. And grinning from ear to ear. I remember touching myself before drifting off to dreamland. I'm so horny I can't stand myself. In my dreams I kept hearing Micah saying he missed me and wanted me. I imagined his strong bare chest coming towards me with his heart beating proudly just for me. I imagined him grinding in between my thighs and feasting on what I was offering him. It was like breathing life into my soul. I saw myself blindfolded and enjoying the ride of my life. He was gripping me and biting me in his own rhythm. There is something about this man that makes me want to lose all of my preconceived morals. Seeing him blindfolded as well having a conversation with my saturation. At one point I heard myself moaning out loud and asking Micah to go deeper writhing for extended orgasms.

I barely slept. I tossed and turned most of the night with my fantasies. I woke up after barely 3 hours of sleep very dismayed, wet and unsatisfied. Hmm cheesecake and wine for breakfast sounds like a wonderful idea Aminah. I need the kind of sex in my dreams to occur in real life. Only although the man in my dreams was who I wanted it from, I need it to come from my husband. The man I know and love. Not some twenty something stranger. I need to continue to devote myself to my work and routine of teaching, reading and writing before I do something I will regret. Last night was fun but its back to work on Monday, Aminah. At least I'll be in the presence of my little crush. I can see him three days a week. That's currently more than I see my husband.

Soul Shaken

These four walls...
I stare into the plainness of it all and I can't breathe
Nothing short of suffocation and I have no justification...
Twas' a night in my dreams, new man in my house
My lover was stirring, all in my blouse
His stature was hung, I imagined him bare
Ravishing my sheets desiring him there
In hopes that my soul would be shaken with care
A special request, a yearning to share
But alas the walls are out of control
It's just these four walls making love to my soul
I want to paint them, even as they close in
But they remove my clothin'... And then...
I, day and night dream, no sleep for the Queen
These four walls making love to me...
The front, back, and one on each side...
Each one movin in on my tide....
The calm before each climax subsides
Pressing my face in each pillow invites
They can't contain themselves getting lost in my sea...
Just these four walls making love to me....

Chapter 5

The Invitation

Going back to Kensington on Monday is going to be awkwardly interesting. I kept my inappropriate night a secret from Sean and my friends. It won't happen again so I don't even want to begin to debate with either of them as to why I did what I did. I drove home in silence and enveloped in the intoxicating scents from the night before. I smelled Micah on me. I felt his embrace around my waist and his breathing on my skin. When I thought of Micah, I thought of the man that couldn't keep his eyes off of me. I was the object of affection. I was his attention and nothing could compare. By no means am I an attention whore. I just would like to be cared for without having to hear my husband's message notifications from outsiders stealing the moments.

I've had so many mixed feelings but as soon as I pulled into the driveway and stepped into my home, I found my husband asleep on the sofa. There was a bouquet of flowers on the kitchen counter that he obviously bought last minute on his way into town at some gas station. All this money and I can't afford a premeditated thought with my husband. I sat down on the couch next to him. He awakened to find me staring at him.

"I love you baby." He said as he sat up to meet and grab my face. "I love you so much" He said again before kissing me. Though having sex with Micah was a tempting fate, my husband hugging and kissing me was undeniably comforting, only now I am instantly riddled with guilt even though nothing sexually occurred.

"Let me get you bags upstairs babe." I said as I maneuvered from his grasp to pick up his luggage.

"Umm actually, I'm headed back out."

"What?"

"Yea, baby, I rushed home to tell you I made the deal in the Hamptons so Candice and I are—"

"Candice?!"

"Babe, you remember Candice from our company's Christmas party. Candice will be joining me in starting the new plans for this deal."

I started to wonder why this kept happening to me, women in their forties, women who seemed to be happy, until the moment they were not. This is my moment. I'm not happy. I love my husband but at this very moment, I am realizing we are more roommates than married. And he is so nose blind that he can't smell another man hot on my trail.

"Sean, you say that you're okay knowing that I'm secure but when I walked in to our home this morning after a birthday evening you were too busy to attend, in the same dress I wore last night, with messy hair and no make-up and you don't even bother to ask where I've been. And here you sit having the audacity to ask me to recall some BITCH I can't place at a Christmas party with the people you are most content and spend more time with than me!"

"Minah, I don't want to fight, I just asked if you remembered her. I won't be alone with her at any point in time. She's just the only co-worker you would be familiar with."

"So I'm supposed to be okay with this? Sean I need you to make me feel wanted and beautiful again. I need you to be around to watch movies with, taste test my new recipes, kiss me on the lips instead of the cheek, make love to me for days on end. I need you!"

"And WE need financial security. I hear you Minah. I won't keep you waiting my love. I promise."

I walked away unmoved by his promises yet again. I trailed upstairs and into the bathroom, locking myself in. Sean came up to tell me goodbye but I was so broken I couldn't move from the bathroom floor. As soon as I heard the side garage door shut I almost felt relieved. Scrambling for my phone I noticed I had a missed message from Micah. I had always naively thought that in order for someone to have an affair, there has to be an inherent problem in the marriage, but all the evidence around me was not only suggesting our lack of communication, but that I personally have developed a sense of insecurity as a result of neglect. I'm not going to make Sean out to look like a monster. He's a good man and I trust that he is working to provide for us. My feelings are more to do with the insecurity of aging, complacency within the marriage, and wanting, even for a little while, to feel beautiful again. My husband's job offers better pussy than me. Moreover, I feel provoked to no longer care how I fill my voids but they need to be filled. Immediately. He gets his rock soft emailing, and texting, and flying from city to city. It's my turn.

"He's leaving again. He's gone." is what I responded to Micah.

Micah called me.

"Hello." I said in between tears.

"Are you okay?" Micah asked, concerned.

"No."

"I don't like hearing you this way. Is it over?"

"I don't know."

"You should come over and get your mind off of things. We can watch movies and I'll grab some wine."

"Come over? To what, your dorm room?" I said with nervous laughter.

Micah's pause was so obvious that I could tell he was blinking his eyes as serious as he could.

"You weren't joking were you? I'm sorry. I didn't mean to offend you."

"I actually live in East Lake so it's not your typical dorm room. I think of it as the apartment I don't have to pay for."

"I understand. I struggled in school believe it or not. I worked three jobs and went to school. My grades always suffered. But it was what I had to do. Mommy and daddy couldn't send their first born off to school, which wasn't the case for their second born but I digress. It's hard. I understand. And again, I'm sorry."

"No apologies necessary Aminah. Just say you'll come over."

"Umm... Sure. Okay. We'll be alone right? I can't risk my career over popcorn and wine."

"Yes, we'll be alone."

"Okay. Cool. I'll see you later."

"Great."

I didn't put it together that East Lake was literally the "center" of campus!! I wore shades and one of my husband's hoodies I always wore when he was away. I parked at a meter that I assumed was free since it was after hours and treaded the parking lot as discretely as possible. I had part of the hoodie covering my face. My height decreased about 2 inches because I'm wearing tennis shoes instead of Louboutin's. No make-up either. After all this isn't a date. Hopefully no one will recognize my MAC free face and 5'3 inch height. I'm all red and puffy anyway. I really look like a student. Lucky for me his room is on the 1st floor. I hate climbing stairs especially in the winter time. Ugh.

I knocked on the door. I waited for about 45 seconds before knocking again, this time with more force. For a moment I began to feel insecure and terrible about my decision to come here. As soon as I changed my mind and turned to leave, I heard Micah jiggling the door knob.

"Hey Aminah, I'm sorry, come in, please. I know its cold out there."

I walked in slowly and silently. I scanned the well-kept apartment. He has good taste. There were complimentary pieces of art that hung on the facing wall and accentuated a large living room window that peered out into an expansive courtyard. Though the scenery was welcoming, I was still feeling anxious and uncertain so I turned right back around facing him.

"You know what Micah. I don't need to be here. I'm going to go home. I'm not really feeling well."

"Would you like some tea? I can fix you some." He said and motioned toward his pots and pans.

"Umm, you don't have to—"

"Please let me take care of you."

"Take care of me?"

"Yes, I'm being hospitable. Stay, and let me do that."

"Oh. Okay. Thank you."

Micah steeped the tea and headed over to the black leather sofa where I was sitting. He took a seat on the adjacent chaise lounge.

"What are we watching?"

"I'll give you a hint. You go for me and I'm taboo. But if you're hard to get I go for you."

"Carmen Jones?"

"Absolutely!"

"Great, I love that movie. I used to watch it all the time because I am obsessed with Dorothy Dandridge. She was so beautiful."

"So are you Aminah. I—mean you have a beautiful spirit."

"Thanks," I said blushing and not even attempting to fight his inappropriateness once more.

"Do you prefer delicate and light desserts or messy desserts with creamy fillings?"

"Excuse me?!"

Micah laughed and laughed hard. I looked up and he was holding a tray of assorted Danish's, fruit with dips, and Chess brownies.

"Oh." I squeezed out, embarrassed by my outburst. "What ever happened to just plain old popcorn? You did promise me popcorn."

"Yes I did, I have that as well but I admit I got the Danish's and fruit from Ocean View for free and I didn't want them to go to waste. The Chess brownies I just felt like making.

"I see. Well, let us partake in the cornucopia of snacks you have created."

He brought them over and placed them on the coffee table and brought two blankets from one of the back rooms and placed one in my lap.

"I don't want you to think I'm putting the moves on you Aminah hence the separate blankets."

"I appreciate the consideration. Thank you."

Micah was wearing basketball shorts, a t-shirt and thick men's socks. I admired his physique up and down. As he sat I inhaled him. He smelled delicious, like Polo Blue, passion fruit, and chocolate. Micah had a face that would stop you in your track with just his smile and his eyes alone. He had smooth brown skin and a low Caesar haircut. His waves were spinning me round' and round'. He was muscular but not over chiseled. Firm and thick would be a better description. I don't see many of his classmates gushing over him like I do. Maybe my taste is different. If he had dimples he would be my husband. How awkward would that be to be a masterpiece and have to get used to the sudden pause in a person's natural expression when looking your way. I don't think he can get enough of the longing gaze he catches me with when I am in his presence. I don't mean to but I can't help it. Of course the blush that accompanies the smile is a dead give-away that I am attracted to him. He is beautiful. I don't know what he sees in me some times. I've always tried to over compensate I guess you can say. Hence the make-up that is a definite must any time I go out and the little bit of weight I've put on that my husband so graciously mentions quite often. Right now my focus has been altered. All I see is this young charming tender piece in front of me. I am confident but I'm not without flaws and right now all of my insecurities have faded into the shadows.

As he began to play the movie I spotted another one of my favorites in his possession.

"Love Jones! Ooo can we watch that one instead? I haven't seen it in years and I've watched Carmen a million times."

"Sure. Whatever you want."

He switched the DVD's out of the player. As he stood in front of me, I continued to admire his strong body.

"If I tell you something, I don't want you to think I'm weird."

He chuckled. "Okay"

"I had a dream about you."

"Really?! My professor has been dreaming about little ol me?!"

"Yes. It was a little wild. I think you put something in my cheesecake last night at The Ocean View."

"No." He laughed. What kind of guy do you think I am? Tell me about your dream."

"Well... In my dream I was kissing you for a while and telling you that I miss you. It was strange and completely inappropriate. I shouldn't have brought it up."

"No, I'm glad you did. I had a dream about you too. A few of them actually. You were holding my head tightly telling me that you missed me as well and you wanted me to enroll in a different course to be able to be with you."

"Is that right? Sounds so stimulating."

"It definitely was."

He sat on the floor next to me. I slid down beside him to sample the desserts but also to feel his warmth and sensual aura next to me. I know I have crossed all lines of professionalism and marital values at this point but I am almost to the brink of tears because I feel like I need to be next to him when I should be next to my husband. The movie began but my thoughts were enveloped in my young suitor. Ya serve a girl dessert and tea and now she's smitten. This is exactly what I was trying to explain to my husband. I don't ask for much. I just need some undivided damn attention sometimes.

"Micah can I ask you something?"

"Sure, shoot."

"That was you that left me that poem wasn't it?"

"Are you going to fail me?"

"Haha, no. Not in the least bit. But was it you?"

"Yes."

"Why would you risk your academic career to flatter me?"

"It was more than just flattery Aminah. You walked into class with so much knowledge and passion but your eyes told me that your heart needed me. Plus my imagination is the most powerful erogenous zone and the way your body walked past me spoke to me in such a way, I had to find the right words to carry on the conversation."

At this very moment, I don't see my husband's face. Up until this second I could see my husband's face and it would prompt me to keep my guard up and only accept Micah's advances to a certain extent and then I would force myself to go home. But he has broken down every ounce of brick and mortar I had against him.

Just as Lorenz Tate was delivering his sexy poem, Blues for Nina, I leaned on Micah's shoulder. Just as I did, he turned to me and I grabbed him by the back of his head to kiss me. He did not refuse this invitation. I don't think even in his mind would he have suggested to take a step into enabling me into adultery. But here we are making out like two teenagers sneaking around in the school's stairwell. He drew close, touching my face. My chin rested in his strong hands. Two tears made their lonely journey down my face. He kissed them.

"What's wrong Aminah?"

"I'm married."

"But we haven't done anything."

"Yet." I said as I pulled him on top of me on the grey carpeted floor. Micah deepened the kiss, sliding his tongue in between my lips. We carried on hot, panting and touching.

I whispered "Maybe you're right, maybe we should stop. Please don't take this moment too seriously. My heart is broken."

He lifted me up to slide my sweatpants and panties off. He licked my throbbing and begging pussy one time, long and stiff tongued. The sensation had me gasping for air. I was totally enveloped in him. His thick tongue made acquaintances with my inner walls. I cried out repeatedly again and again until he was sure that my body couldn't wait much longer.

He then pulled his member out of his shorts and said "Minah, moments are meant to be embraced." He then took my hand to grasp a hold of it. "This may be our only opportunity. Just take it...."

Take It...

While he's up in the early morning & late night hours

exchanging his number

I want to give you my love

until you fall victim to a sweet slumber

I want to suck each lip of yours because I'll enjoy the way

they kiss back

I won't mind picking up where he lacked

I will wrap my hands firm around your throat and pull

your hair back

He can't leave work alone, he'll never be content with

just you, shame

Nothing I can potentially say

that won't make me sound the same

So let's start by introducing my name...

Over... And... Over again

I need to punish you for making me wait

until he fucked up woman

But don't worry my dear,

I'll touch you where it hurts the most

We'll raise glasses in the midnight hour... Toast

I just want to give you passion, enough to keep your

phone off the ringer

To not waste your better years and allow you to linger

Just allow me to insert these two fingers

Pounding my fists on the wall because your body makes me excited

Softly curvaceous and since I'm invited...

I'm prepared to go face deep in your twat to make sure you tweet... No mention

And then immediately place you strategically on top of me... Ascension

For your newly slanted frame, give him my condolences

For you my dear I'm glad I could be of assistance...

Solaces

However with this one night,

I hope you will offer me forever

I can't promise you I won't disrespect you, no not never

But I can promise that I am not like the latter

I promise there is no ounce of me that

desires to see you sadder

Fuck him he can't help it so let me help you right now during this time

I want to fuck you in a way that will make you mine

I want to suck each lip of yours

because I'll enjoy the way they kiss back

I won't mind picking up where he lacked

Just take it...

Chapter 6

What Have I Done?

A powerful orgasm rolled up through my body, warm and all-consuming, I shuddered and whimpered as Micah continued to fuck me. I lost count of which round we were on as sparks of sensation coursed through my veins, drawing the orgasm out longer as he hit the perfect spot within me. Micah's thrust was deep as he groaned. I panted and moaned too knowing that he was about to cum. *I have been held captive by a quiet monster and made to feel powerless.* I know that this encounter is not by some divine intervention, indicating I am not meant for my husband and that this indiscretion will result in Micah and I falling madly in love with each other and he'll whisk me away to eternal bliss.

There is something intrinsically wrong with the whole notion. I know for a fact that there is no perfect spouse and I too am far from perfection, but no one else knew that. My husband got the support and love he needed and my friends as well.

But what about me? I was the epitome of perfection to them but I was suffering on the inside. No one asks, "Are you okay?" No one says, "Talk to me." No, I am the ear and the voice of reason. I kept my anguish and frustrations to myself at first because I didn't have a choice and now I remain silenced to preserve my own self-image. This isn't just about sex. This is an escape. This is my mental release from the ordinary. Children act out when they are not paid enough attention or when they are given way too much attention but no understanding.

My acting out is from never being heard. Micah listened. He let me vent and now he is fucking me into delirium. *He is my new drug and I don't want to go to rehab. I am completely captivated,* I thought as I kneeled in front of him to perform fellatio to get him hard once more. And did I perform. The tongue tricks I was doing were award winning. I don't know what's come over me. This is the fourth time we've had sex since last night and I can't get enough of his mouth, his excitement, his tongue, his chest, his voice in my ear telling me how I feel on his dick. Oh and that dick. That beautifully exquisite member. His dick was my mentor. If at any moment he sensed I wasn't enjoying him to the fullest, he would say *"Teach me Minah. Tell me what you want me to do to you."* I had never been more relaxed, carefree and so flexible in my life. Micah brings that out of me. I couldn't hide my pleasure and was very proud of my skill as I heard him moan out loud. My husband is not so forthcoming with his sexual reactions. I would hold my breath during our encounters, savoring each moment with Micah, praying that it could last because I knew I shouldn't do it again. Every time we would cum and fall asleep, one of us would awaken the other with pleasure. I'd feel him begin tracing my clit with his fingers and then entering my pussy digitally. He would use his tongue to stroke intently and suckle my clit creating a delicious explosion. *"You taste so good Minah."* He said as he continued sliding his fingers across my wet slit.

Whenever he would penetrate me after an orgasm, I'd define this as part ecstasy and part torture. I wanted to scream with the sexual electric shock he had radiating within me. Equivalent to when I would give him head, he would cum and I would keep sucking and swallowing. I begged him to touch me wherever I needed it most. He was relentless and merciless in my request. I believe that my breasts were his favorite feature on my body. Feeling the soft firmness of them turned him on and he left each one wet with his mouth. He enjoyed watching me grab them as he continued to fuck me. *"I'm going to take you Minah. Know that I want to please you."* He said with so much conviction. He turned me over on my knees and pulled me close to him.

He inserted his warm dick inside of me once more and wrapped his strong hands around my neck. *Deeper.* I said as he began pounding me from behind. Micah rose at this point and grabbed both of my round apple cheeks for leverage. He rocked harder and harder as we panted, sweating, and moaning. My muscles clinched deep inside and released one final orgasm which gripped Micah's swollen dick like a mighty fist as a tantalizing wave of pleasure overcame him. He pulled out of me swiftly and commenced to climax. We slept all day Sunday. We hadn't even got up to hydrate ourselves after such an extensive fuck session. I felt like I died. I guess a part of me did. When I was sleeping, I didn't hear anything, I didn't feel anything. I was numb, satisfied and confused.

Though it was a passion I had built up inside of me, I didn't know how to approach the aftermath. My marriage isn't truly over. *Should I feel bad for not saying anything and just relishing in the moment? What if there are moments plural? I am completely addicted at this point and I don't know if this night could just be the only instance.* Monday's embrace welcomed us as we lay in each other's arms. Lucky for me, Monday's classes were canceled due to flooding. Micah got up to go to the bathroom. I heard water running so I assumed he was taking a shower. He came back into the room dry and in his boxers and grazed his hand across my face.

"I don't know why you wear make-up. You are flawless. Good morning beautiful."

"Mornin, handsome." I replied.

"I've drawn you a bath angel. It's ready when you are. I'm going to go make us something to eat."

When I sat up, reality pulled me right back down. I didn't want to face the day. I furiously blinked back tears of frustration with myself. It was all the strength I could summon to shake my hazy state and slide out of the bed and into the tub of warm water and bubbles Micah had drawn for me. I had completely broken down. I ran water simultaneously so that Micah could not hear my soft whimpers and sniffling. *What am I doing here? What am I doing?* I did nothing to keep at bay the situation I'm in. I walked further and further into this sea of lust and deceit thinking that the inviting waters would clear my mind, release suffering and heartache and make it all go away. It did not. It has thrived and evolved in vivid colors. My mind drifted. Micah knocked at the door inquiring on my state and why I locked the door. "I'll be out in a minute." I said as I emerged from the tub and wrapped myself in a towel. I pulled my hair up into a messy bun and unlocked the door to go back to Micah's bedroom.

He met me there with a tray which held a glass of orange juice and a plate with scrambled egg whites, yogurt and wheat toast. "I hope you don't mind the yogurt instead of a breakfast meat. I don't eat pork and I'm all out of turkey bacon."

"It's okay. This is perfect."

"Can I get you anything else?" He said eagerly.

"No, Micah this is fine."

"Okay." He said as he peered down. "I just want you to know I'm not going to share what happened between us with anyone Aminah. My only desire is your comfort in knowing that."

"Yes, I believe you." I think that most men Micah's age would be reaping the bragging rights of not only fucking a 40 year old woman but his own teacher to boot. Part of me is waiting for him to revert to a young man that wasn't ready for a woman like me, to use every opportunity he can to tell someone our business and come to the conclusion that he will never trust any woman married or single based off of what I've done in my own union.

My mind drifted and I got lost in this lustful fantasy made reality. The thought of disappointing my husband twisted my stomach. The thought of my student becoming my lover and how I had jeopardized my marriage sickened me even more. Micah's words were comforting to hear, but I knew that the first time would not be the last time I would sleep with him, therefore it was unclear from the start just how long this could possibly remain a secret. *How long could I keep up the charade? My husband will come home and though I do not plan on admitting the ugly truth, how many lies can I come up with to hide where I'm going, where I've been, why I may smell like cologne? Oh my goodness what have I done?*

To My Lover

Why do you always leave me wanting you more?

Controversial and scandalous and yet I adore

You and the blessing between your legs

that sways like a mighty oak

Lifting me into oblivion equivalent to dope

I am completely consumed

I remain pleasantly doomed

You woke me up with the softest of kisses

In between my hips then gave me three wishes

You've surely granted me more wishes than three

I know I've given you enough to judge my decree

You're something artistic, yes you are gifted

And like my marriage, my mind drifted

It's a man down situation

In reference to your penetration

Don't get me wrong baby I can hold my own

I am Aminah, I'm 40 years grown

But I am admittedly losing this battle of moan

It's difficult to be strong when your backs blown

Sometimes I can be accident prone

But it's not my fault I need my bottom half sewn

Neighbors panic because I can't stop screaming

Maybe they'll think I'm just nightmare dreaming

Ooooooooooo....Ahhhhhhhhh

That climax with no replica

I'm waving my white flag, put down the hazardous cones

You have officially murdered all of my erogenous zones

Plan the services, I like yellow flowers

Life escaped me after 4 hours

The lightening has struck, the rain is pouring

The crime has been committed, and now it is morning

Chapter 7

Hump Day

If I ever prayed for variety I received more than I bargained for. Sean would make his debut at home and he'd be in front of the computer almost as soon as he got there, as usual. He has noticed however that I haven't been wearing any make up lately, that my bedroom heels are now my work heels and that I've been adding a lot more color to my wardrobe. I had begun lying to him and telling him I was going out with friends but I was with Micah. It's not like my husband would be concerned enough to check behind my words and ask my friends directly if I was with them so I didn't tell my friends about my never ending rendezvous with Micah. Our ongoing affair made things even more awkward than before. It's carried into the second semester, my Great Books II course and I believe that his peers are noticing more and more.

"Class thank you for showing up today despite the awful rain out there and happy Wednesday to you. The author we are covering today is Laura Esquivel and the idea of romanticism in the 20th century in comparison to the century previous. We will take a look at the styles on a broader scope yet intensely personal in focus, Laura Esquivel's *Like Water For Chocolate* which tells the story of Tita De La Garza, the young lady who desires marriage but is forbidden so that she could take care of her ailing mother. The man she is smitten by pursues her sister in an attempt to always be near Tita and is so for over 22 years."

Micah raises his hand. There is no way I can ignore him. I see him here today and all I can think about is us laughing in the rain, slow dancing in the red room, surrounded by darkness feeling the safest I've ever felt and then having incredible sex. These thoughts make me want him more.

"Yes Micah?"

"How does it end?"

"I'm sorry? How does what end?"

"Like Water for Chocolate, how does it end? Does the guy get to finally have Tita all to himself or does he just continue an affair with her while he's married to her sister?"

"Umm, I don't want to ruin the story for you. For those of you that have not seen the movie or read the book, please do not skip ahead. The point of these exercises is to test your analytical skills. For those of you who know the story, do watch the movie and read the book over because what you think you knew before may surprise you."

I could have killed Micah for making such a statement. If I was one of his peers I would be able to tell he was fucking me by him asking that question and by the way he's always looking at me. God, I miss him. After class I gathered my things and noticed another note face down on the desk where I found the poem.

"Meet me at the library."

Micah led the way to the restroom on the third floor of the Kensington Library and walked into the women's entrance with no hesitation. I had the chance to renege on my decision to meet him here and I had a few 'neverminds' on the tip of my tongue but I looked around to see not one soul on that floor. I walked in slowly and he jerked me into his arms.

"You smell like nutmeg and honey. Sweet and mysterious." He said as he kissed me. It was hot and demanding. "I need that honey to drip down my chin."

I found myself melting into him, sinking into his touch, seduced by the taste of him and how he so expertly commanded me.

"Fuck me." I said as I began clawing at his zipper yanking it down and he reached under my electric blue skirt to hike it up and slide my panties off. I haven't worn a skirted suit since

before my husband and I were married and colored anything in ages.

"Mmmm, yes." Micah said as he leaned over towards the door to lock it. It was impossible to gather any moments of clarity when he kissed me, I immediately got on my knees allowing him to begin thrusting into my wet mouth. When he couldn't resist me anymore Micah lifted me up and turned me around. He thumbed his way in my pussy to navigate his dick into it. He enjoyed the way I fucked my ass back against it. I was trying desperately to keep quiet over the vibrating pulses that suddenly consumed me and all preconceived judgments were long gone. We were spontaneous and animalistic even.

"Why do you fuck me so good baby."

"Because this pussy is what my dick was made for baby. You feel me? You feel all this inside of you? This is how you make me feel when I'm sitting in class. I should punish you for making me feel so crazy and you can't be all mine."

"Punish me baby."

Micah took a black blindfold out of his pocket and wrapped it around my eyes. There was complete and total blackness. He then took a second scarf and wrapped my wrists with it. He propped his hoodie underneath my knees to protect them from the floor. This was premeditated. *How the hell did he know I would follow him up here for this?*

"Micah what is about to ha—"

"Shut up." he said while covering my mouth. He began to drill me again from behind. The feeling was so overwhelming between the kinky talk and his action. He smacked me hard on the ass and ordered me to say things I have never said. In the beginning it was different and I wasn't sure if I could be compliant to his wishes. But as time went on the words flowed like water and so did the cum between my legs. Roleplaying was exciting and even more enticing because it was technically in the open. My husband is always so reserved. He wouldn't be caught dead taking initiative like this to please me.

"Micah I'm cummmmminnnnng!" I said vibrating and completely weakened. He slowed his buck to firm continuous thrusts until he pulled out and came on top of me. I turned around and he held me close to his chest. "Do you hear that Aminah?"

"What?"

"It's my heart beating for you."

"Micah, please don't say things like that. Especially if you don't mean it."

"Oh but I do mean it Minah. You're changing my world. I could be with you any day all day. You're my oxygen when I can't breathe and my mood stabilizer when I don't think I can get through the day. Please have me. I want to be your man."

"Micah I am married."

"What?! How can you say that?! How can you argue you're married when we've been fucking for the past six months?!"

"Micah please keep your voice down."

"Yea or what? You don't want the faculty to know you've been having an affair with some kid?! Your student?! Aminah baby I feel like I'm falling in love with you but there are three legs to this table and the unbalance is killing me. Don't you want me?"

"Yes. I mean no. I don't know Micah. I thought we were just having fun."

"Fun? Okay. "

"Micah don't be like that." I said as I got redressed.

"No I understand. You only wanted me to kill time. You're going to go back to a husband that doesn't love you and I am forced to walk away from what might have been the best thing that's ever happened to me."

After dressing in silence, Micah turned and left from the bathroom. I stood there collecting my thoughts and realizing that not only was I taking advantage of my marriage but of someone that really did care. Or so I thought.

Chapter 8

Grass Ain't Green No More

Morning meetings suck. It's 7 am and I don't teach a class today until 5:30 pm! Plus I am so in my thoughts about what I am doing outside of work. I am cheating on my husband. I am cheating on my husband with my student. If my colleagues knew at this very moment, I would be fired indefinitely. That is the reality of the situation. I leaned back in my chair with my pen cap in my mouth. As I twirled it my mind continued to do backflips. I couldn't deny the feeling between my legs. How can this situation be making me horny? Surely I have had enough. I broke Micah's heart and I want very badly to fix my mistake. The more I pondered the more I felt wetness in between my thighs followed by an insane itch that could not be ignored. I excused myself to the restroom and locked the door behind me. What the fuck is going on? I must have a yeast infection or something.

I pulled my pants and panties down and divided my legs to inspect myself. This is definitely a yeast infection. Gross! I hate these things. Thank God I carry wet wipes. Wiping the area clean, I immediately discard the wipe, zipped my pants, washed my hands and speed dialed my OB-GYN.

"Yes, Miss Goodwin, we can see you today."

"It's Mrs. and thank you."

Haha. Wow, did I really just correct her on using the appropriate prefix to my name? Clearly I am not acting anything like a "Mrs." these days. Walking back to the meeting room I noticed everyone leaving so I turned around and headed to my car. My path was swift because I am miserable beneath these dress pants. The itchiness is as annoying as a mosquito bite. I just want to go home, take the medicine, take a shower, and get in bed. I picked up my cell phone and speed dialed the doctor.

"Yes Amanda, this is Mrs. Goodwin again. Cancel my appointment, if anything changes, I will reschedule."

As I hung up for the second time I could see Micah out of the corner of my eye. He was sitting thigh to thigh in the stairwell with some skinny heffa sporting a 22 inch hair weave... I'm estimating... And a dress so tight I could see all her parts. I could feel my body begin to shake. I walked over to them and I saw him trace the outline of her lips with his thumb. How dare he?! Who is this little trollop? I demanded answers but I realized I hadn't opened up my mouth to speak nor had they separated airways long enough to notice me staring at them. Let me just go. If I make a scene, the Vice Provost down the hall will surely see me and inquire on what is the matter. I carried on my swift pace to my car, deleted Micah's number out of my phone and slowly backed out of Kensington. I went straight to the pharmacy to buy some Monistat for my little situation. As I pull into the driveway at home I notice my husband is not here which a good thing this time. Walking in, I kicked off my shoes and headed straight for the bathroom. After showering and inserting the medication I fell asleep in no time.

My phone is dead and I plan to enjoy these moments of clarity and solitude. While placing it on the charger, I resist the temptation to devise any kind of devious escape plan. I just need hot tea and my blanket. I don't need a man tonight. Not even my own husband.

I woke up suddenly at 3am to find myself disarrayed on the couch and panties soaked. Oh Dear God this is horrible. I bought the three day treatment. Usually after day one it begins to clear up. Seriously? A woman goes through so much just being a damn woman. Damn. In about 10 more years I'll be dealing with menopause. Dear Jesus! Since my phone has now been charged to 100%, I decide to call Laurisse because Lord knows that chick can talk. Laurisse works midnights as a Housekeeping Manager at a hotel downtown. She ain't doin shit. I retrieved my phone from the charger. Zero missed calls. That's not surprising. Micah is still with that floozy and my husband is with his mistress as well, otherwise known as his job. Dialing Laurisse I decided to put her on speaker while I go to the bathroom and do another thorough cleaning.

"Hello?!"

"Hey girl. Wassup with you?"

"Girl, don't be callin me at 3 in the morning talkin about wassup. I thought somebody died."

"You always think somebody died Laurisse. Haha. Anyway heffa what you up to, you at work? Hardly workin?"

"You already know. Haha! What you doin up? What's wrong?"

"Nothing, just needed to hear a familiar voice."

"Where's Sean?"

Without thinking and from what seems like second nature I replied, "I don't know."

"What do you mean you don't know where your husband is Minah?"

"I meeaaan I know he is working, but I don't know where he is LAURISSE... Shit, what's with the third degree? I called to check on you and you're asking me about my got damn husband."

"No bitch, correction, I asked you what was wrong and by wrong, I was referencing your ABSENT hubby. No third degree, just went right for the usual source."

"I'm not sad and I'm not even lonely tonight. I just wanted to kick it on the phone with my home girl, if you don't mind."

"Mmmmhmm okay Minah... Okay."

"Damn, okay so back to MY original question, how the hell are you?!"

"Haha, I'm good. I am sick of cleaning these nasty ass hotel rooms but nonetheless it is a paycheck and a free room if I ever need one. Which reminds me, can you watch AJ and Lia this weekend?"

"Sure." I said while rolling my eyes.

"Are you rolling your eyes?"

"Yes. Yes I am."

"I knew it!"

"Oooo Psychic."

"I can sense something is wrong with your ass but you're not telling me."

"If I tell ya, I'll have to kill ya."

"Oh come on Aminah, you never dish. Spill it!"

"Have you ever thought about stepping out on Deandre?"

"Hell yea! Every time he come in the house with them dirty ass Jordan's on after I slaved in the kitchen on my off day. But then he dickmotizes me and all is well with the world."

"Shut up Laurisse! Dickmotize? Who says that?"

"Well obviously not you Dr. Aminah Goodwin." She mocked.

"What is 'Dickmotize' Laurisse?"

"Okay, it's when you are mad at Sean but then he fucks the shit out of you and you don't remember what he did to make you mad and whatever he does thereafter it won't even matter because you know what he got in them pants. It's the kind of sex that has you cooking eggs and bacon in the morning right after an orgasm while your body is still trembling. Yessssss Honey! Wooooooooo!!" She exclaimed.

"Thank you for that thorough explanation, Laurisse, thank you."

"You're welcome girl, you know I got you. So wassup, you thinkin about steppin out on Sean? Oh my goodness DID you step out on Sean? "I don't believe it, Ms. Goodie Two Shoes is an adulterer!"

"No." (Lying). "It's just something that has crossed my mind every now and then but nothing I will actually pursue. I love my husband."

"Do you think he is being faithful to you? I mean, he is always at work. Do you think he considers it too?"

"I don't know."

"Look Aminah, we are grown. I don't want to say old because we are still fly. If you're feeling like you're lusting after other men, you need to talk to your husband. However, if you do go after another man, don't get caught."

"Why do you say that?"

"Because you'll make us all look bad. Haha!"

"Goodnight fool!"

"Night girl."

After having that conversation with Laurisse, despite her own flaws, I don't believe she will be able to understand what is going on in my life right now. I know she damn sure wouldn't support it. Hell, I don't even support it and it's my own pussy reaping the benefits. A true man's approach is based on a woman's presentation. I'm probably presenting too much these days. I haven't heard from my husband all day. For shits and giggles I decided to call him.

(Voicemail) "You have reached the voicema---"

Dead. What else is new? Just like our marriage... DEAD.

Friday came sooner than I had hoped. I cancelled my Friday class which I am sure the students are glad of. I decided to go to the doctor. This yeast infection is not disappearing without a fight and how does that look the next time I have sex. On my way to see Dr. Seigul I made a mani-pedi appointment. Why waste the day?

As I walk in the doctor's office, Olivia, the nurse practitioner took me right back.

"How are you Mrs. Goodwin? How is Mr. Goodwin?"

"Everyone is fine thanks Olivia."

"What seems to be the problem?"

"I have a yeast infection that has got to go to hell."

"Haha. Gotcha. Okay well, let's just do a quick exam with Dr. Seigul and see what we can do for you and get you on your way."

"That'll be great. Thanks."

Dr. Seigul walks in just as Olivia is walking out.

"Hi Dr. Seigul."

"Hello again Olivia. Hey there Mrs. Goodwin. Welcome back. What's going on?"

"Well I-"

"She has a yeast infection." Olivia blurted out.

"Thank you Olivia, that'll be all."

"Sure thing Dr. Seigul! Bye Mrs. Goodwin!"

"Bye Olivia."

"That girl is too damn cheery." Dr. Seigul muttered.

"Haha."

"Alright dear, let's lie back."

"I laid back in the chair and put my legs in the stirrups. I hate these things. I hate exposing my snootch to these strangers."

"I'm going to take some samples Aminah just to rule out any STI's, STD's etc."

"Okay, no worries."

"Same sexual partner for the last 6 months?"

Technically this answer should be no. I can't remember the last time my husband and I made love. I really contemplated on telling her the truth. It's not like confidentially, she can tell my husband anything. But alas, I continued to live a lie and replied, "Yes".

After about 10 minutes of swabbing and examining Dr. Seigul was off in the hall again and I was in the empty exam room. I could have heard a pin drop. The uncomfortable silence prompted me to pray.

'Lord, I thank you for everything you have done for me. Whatever is your will is your way. Please forgive my selfish and sinful needs. I ask you for your mercy and guidance. Amen.' By the end of my prayer, Olivia's cheery ass comes back in the room.

"Mrs. Goodwin, what you have is not a yeast infection. You have an STI called Trichomoniasis, most commonly known as 'Trich'........"

Why Me?

Usually I am the only one on point with apologies
Believe me it is not to amuse and appease
I am being genuine and my actions back my tongue
If you needed a performance I'm the last song sung
But I've desired the return of my investment for so long
I know I need to take ownership, I know I was wrong
But I feel that with my husband I will never
hold the same recognition
Maybe I'll catch it during intermission
I'm sorry I've said too much
Make believing things not within my clutch
Because it was my husband that made promises but didn't
follow through first
Always been blamed for my counteraction and it's other's
wounds I nursed
I don't want to make anyone mad
But it's like I've never been able to address
the issue when I'm sad
So why me?
Why am I the one that gets the punishment?
What if my husband isn't even surprised?
No signs of astonishment
After ten years is he still trying to figure me out?

Going the "do your own thing but keep me" route?

I hope he knows that I was never his enemy,

maybe I should look in the mirror

Stop playing so many games so I can see things clearer

But my judgment was clouded and now I'm paying my dues

Just know my dear husband I was waiting for you

Your strong ambition was accepted and often encouraged

You'll probably say I knew the deal

but now I'm feeling discouraged?

Just know that the problem was never who you are

I loved you even from afar

I'm sorry you will now know about my current addiction

The problem is so simple it can't be written in fiction

I needed my husband and as usual he wasn't there

I feel like my actions deserve the electric chair

My husband made promises but didn't follow through first

Always been blamed for my counteraction and it's other's

wounds I nursed

So why me?

Chapter 9

Forgive Me for I Have Sinned

I trembled with embarrassment. I was shaking with the fear of having to explain this to my unsuspecting husband. What do I say? Hey honey, not only have I been having an affair for months but he gave me an STD. Will you still love me? How could you love me? I'm disgusting. I broke our vows to satisfy the lust in my eyes but I love you? Does that even make sense? Oh my God.

"Aminah, there is quite a bit of the Trich so we are going to have to treat it immediately and aggressively. I will give you two antibiotics here and give you a prescription to fill at the pharmacy."

"This can't be. This has got to be wrong. He never came inside of me and-and we are always careful."

"Mrs. Goodwin, you know just as well as I do that his semen is not the reason you've contracted this. Unprotected sex is. You're lucky you're not pregnant too."

"Okay I said quietly." I knew that.

"Please get dressed and knock when you are ready for the antibiotics."

"Will do." I whispered.

I sat in silence. I wanted to kill myself. I would rather die than have to face my husband. I clothed myself and propped myself back on the table. I sat momentarily and forgetting that I was supposed to alert Olivia to come back with the medication.

With my face low and stride slow I shuffled myself to the door and knocked for Olivia to return. She did and administered two pills and a cup of water. "Are you okay Mrs. Goodwin?"

"Yes, I'm fine Olivia."

"Okay, well if you need a good divorce attorney I—"

"I won't be needing one. What makes you think I need a divorce attorney?"

"I—I'm sorry," Olivia stuttered and started towards the door. "You're all set Mrs. Goodwin. Andrea will meet you up front to set your follow-up appointment. "

Upon leaving the doctor's office I was numb and confused. At this point who do I confront for doing this to me? My husband or my lover? Who do I be angry at? I'm too old to be walking around burnin! Oh dear God. I wanted to tell my husband about Micah but I hadn't. I wanted to break it off with Micah and I hadn't done that either. I know I deserved this and it could have been HIV. But how the hell do I even bring this up in conversation. After reading up on the disease and by my own calculation this is something that doesn't typically lie dormant and if that is the case than this couldn't have been caused by my husband. We haven't had sex in months. We've been too mad at each other or he's gone. The only other partner I've had has been Micah.

I got home and I saw my husband's SUV was in the driveway. "Shit!" I have no time to even prepare a better attitude before I walk in the door. I need to wipe the worry and tears from my face. I called Micah to let him know he gave me Trich. After our last encounter, I wasn't sure if he even wanted anything to do with me.

"Hello."

"Hey Minah."

"Micah, there's no easy way to say this but I just came back from the doctor's office for what I thought was a yeast infection. Micah you gave me Trich."

"Sorry."

"What the fuck do you mean, sorry?"

"I said sorry Aminah damn. Why didn't you accuse your husband first? Oh yea, right, because he wasn't fucking you, I was."

"You fucking asshole."

"You loved every bit of me Minah, admit it. Now you're mad because you have to explain this to the man you took vows with. The man that leaves you for weeks on end and the man you leave to come away with me. I'm falling in love with you and you just let me. I knew you belonged to another, so I resorted to other women. Yes. During the nights I needed you and you were wrapped up in another man's arms. I cooked breakfast for other women after I spent the night fucking them and before sending them on their way. Yes I subjected myself to other women that I barely knew without protection but you didn't stop me from fucking the shit out of you to put a condom on or to salvage your lifeless marriage. I don't even know why I'm apologizing to you. I would've spent the rest of your days loving and cherishing you the way you were supposed to be treated."

"You don't know that?!" I erupted. "Do you know how many times my husband has said I'm sorry. There are 365 days in a year and he is gone for more than half of that time. He's sorry. He forgets my birthday after promising me that he will be back in time to celebrate with me. He's sorry. On Valentine's Day, he sees the decorations in stores and on the calendar but somehow he manages to forget to get me something. He's sorry. His phone died after being on it for hours on end but not having enough power for my call. He's sorry. He forgot that I like lilies and not roses. He's sorry. He forgot, he forgot, he forgot and he's sorry. Micah I cannot and will not accept one more 'sorry'. I don't have any room left in my heart."

"That makes two of us." Micah said and then I heard a faint click.

The dial tone I heard after Micah hung up infuriated me but I had to pull it together before walking into my house. I walked in and there were candles everywhere. There were big lily bouquets all over the counter tops and wine on ice.

"Baby, it's the middle of the day. What is all of this?"

"Minah, I know I haven't been the perfect man and you've been pretty sick of me lately, but I love you. I don't want to lose you. I know you're unhappy but I want to change that. I'm off for a little while and I want to spend every moment with you. "

I stood shocked and horrified. He wants to spend every moment with me? Now?!

'Sean, baby, I've waited so long to hear you say that. I love you too and I'm looking forward to you being here for a while."

"It won't just be for a while baby. That's what I came home to tell you. While Candice and I were out for this last deal she was trained into my current position. I got a higher paid position with less travel. Much less. I'm home baby."

"Oh my god Sean that's great!" I exclaimed with open arms as I fought back tears."

"Babe, don't cry, no need to."

"These are happy tears." I said, lying. When I released him from my grasp Sean kissed me and kept kissing me initiating sex.

"Baby, I have some chaffing and I don't really want to have sex, it's going to hurt."

"I'll be gentle babe." Sean said as he started to remove my clothes and his pants.

Nooooo! I know the doctor gave me a dose of the medicine that I need to get rid of the Trich but surely it hasn't coursed through my system yet. There was no more debating at this point with my husband. It was either have sex with him or ruin the moment and tell him the truth.

I had sex with my husband that night. It was excruciating and sad to say the least. I finally have his full attention but it's too late. I've already given my body to another. And though he has given me this infection, I still don't know if I'm able to stop wanting Micah. I know he's angry with me as I with him. But it's almost like I'm able to make more sense of our relationship and my feelings for him than my own husband thrusting between my legs, pleasuring himself to an unknown fate. Time will tell soon I'm sure.

Micah on the other hand, I don't know when he won't be upset with me and it shouldn't matter. But what he said stuck with me. *I'm falling in love with you and you just let me.* Could he really love me? This is not Jamaica and my name is not Stella. I feel more like Aminah the Whore at this point.

You Just Let Me

If only you would let me love you the way that you need to be

I listened to your cries and fed you when you were hungry

I delivered what has been so deprived from your soul

I picked up the pieces when you were beyond my console

If only you would let me love you

the way that you need to be loved

If you wouldn't disregard my heart, ignored it and shoved

I should've known you would go back to him

How can I compete with your husband?

But I thought in between sweltering sheets

And the late night phone calls requesting my lap as your seat

Satisfying each other as if our lives were to end

I'm in love with you damn, how much time did I spend?

Loving the mornings waking up in each other's arms

Hoping I wasn't just another link, lucky charms

Baby I know you've been hurt on various

unbearable occasions

But I was able to whisk you away

to an abandoned constellation

In a short time I gave you the stars in the galaxy

What's unfortunate is that you just let me....

Chapter 10

Who Are You?

As I gazed into the mirror I didn't recognize the woman's reflection before me. I imagined my husband's reaction to my affair.

"How could you have done this to me, to us? Who are you and who did I marry?" With tears in his eyes, my husband shouted and screamed these questions at me and all the while, I stood there shaking, in shock, not knowing what to say that would make what I had done, right. I was a cheater.

I realize that nothing in that moment would have given him the support and comfort that either of us was looking for. I'll become the nightmare he can't wake up from. I should tell him about the Trich. Maybe I'll just crush up a lil of the antibiotic and blend it up in his smoothie.

The question that I kept asking myself was "Why?" Why did I cheat on him? Why would I do such a thing to a man who was caring, funny and generous? It wasn't like he beat on me or anything like that.

He would be within his rights to divorce me. He might even attempt to take my life. No one judged me more harshly than I did, and even now, although I assume that my husband would be angry enough to tear down the walls of our two story home because of my actions, I am not completely positive it will play out this way.

I read something about how cheating women are more likely to stray as they are seeking emotional fulfillment, an improvement to their self-esteem and romance. When women cheat it depends on how fulfilled they feel in their marriage and how they identify that fulfillment. Women also are usually the partner that seeks to be fulfilled outside of their marriage first.

After years of denying that if women are truly in love that they would not cheat, I finally came to the understanding of what drove me to cheat and why I had stepped into the shoes of a throng of unfaithful women. Micah was selling fantasy stock and I bought a hundred shares.

I crept to the downstairs bathroom and called Laurisse to tell her I submitted to Micah's advances. I called Celeste first but she didn't pick up. Laurisse wasn't surprised and she remained very non-judgmental until I told her about the 'Trich'.

"Girl what the fuck? Now you didn't tell me yall were having unprotected sex?"

"Does it matter?" I said.

"Well, I guess not but girl are you gonna tell him?"

"I have to Laurisse."

"No you don't! Girl you better crush them antibiotics up and put it in his smoothie!"

I laughed hysterically. This is not funny. Not in the least bit but Laurisse's advice to resolve my situation was exactly what I had been thinking. I don't want to admit this to my husband. But I don't want to hurt him either. I couldn't live with myself if he took severely ill because he isn't treated. I need to put on my big girl panties and tell him. Tomorrow!

Chapter 11

Unraveled

It's Monday afternoon once again and I could care less about the agenda of the meeting. Dr. Kelli Beckett sat across from me staring so hard I was tempted to climb over the cherry wood and slice her face off. She caught Micah embracing me after my lecture a few weeks ago. She hasn't brought it up, she just stares. She knows I'm married and ever since that day, she's had it in for me. If she had something to say, now would be the time because I am ready to pounce.

There was nothing at this meeting that could possibly grasp my attention long enough when I knew my fate was about to be transformed. I have made up my mind. Today is the day I tell my husband that I have had an affair and that he may need to get himself checked for STD's. I'm mortified. Every time I think about it, I cry. Something did resonate with me that my unhappiness with my husband will finally be in the light.

In preparation for class at 5:30 I decided to hide in the computer lab next to Carroll to prepare my lecture notes. I haven't heard from Micah since our blow out. I can't say I don't miss him but there is no way I can cater to his temper tantrum because he is not getting his way. I have bigger fish to fry and our carelessness is the root of my dilemma.

I logged into the computer and just as I did I shrieked in terror. There was a picture of Micah and me at his apartment having sex. There I was spread apart wearing nothing but my Louboutin's! I hurriedly deleted the photo and logged into another computer. There I was again, this time receiving my lover from the side with the heel of my red bottoms in his mouth. I logged into another, and another and another, each one displaying some intimate explicit photograph of me and Micah and me with my wedding ring blinging in all the photos. I've realized that throughout the whole time I was with Micah, I never took it off. I looked up at the clock and there was only a short window of time to delete all of them. Next to the clock rests a security camera. I threw my scarf over it and continued to delete the photos from each desktop. When I was finished I swiftly walked down the sidewalk to enter Carroll Hall. "That idiot played me." I said to myself. I walked into my classroom and awaited Micah's arrival so that I could question his motives for exploiting us this way. He's trying to ruin me! I stood fuming, as one by one my students began trickling in and taking their seat. None of whom were Micah. Instead I noticed a small slip of paper atop the desk of his usual seat. I tried to act as if everything was normal and began my lecture. I slowly made my way over to Micah's empty chair without trying to be too obvious. I picked the piece of paper up slowly and gracefully. It read **"You should have just let me love you. You should've just told Sean the truth."**

"Umm class, you'll have to excuse me, I have an emergency situation I need to tend to."

I sped out of the classroom and down the hall, my heels pounding the linoleum with each step as I made my way out the door, to my car. I don't know what Micah plans to do next after he's pulled that degrading stunt in the computer lab. I have a feeling he is going to try to tell my husband everything.

Driving home I prepared my speech. "Sean, we need to talk." That's as far as I got. I have no idea where to go from there. I could lead with how absent he's been but to end with I'm having an affair and I have an STI would surely override my argument. I'd be the poster child for hypocrisy and adultery. Micah just might be bluffing. Then again, maybe he is not. He already stooped as low as posting those pictures. Who knows what other media files of us he's been keeping in his possession.

I saw my husband's car in the driveway and it was the only car. Maybe I beat Micah here. I locked my car doors and ran inside.

"Sean!" I yelled.

No response.

"Sean honey!"

Nothing.

I peered around the living room into the den and saw Sean standing completely still.

"Sean?"

Sean turned around slowly and Micah stood to the side of him with a 9mm in his hands pointed at my husband's head. Sean was holding a crumpled photo of me and my lover in a completely carnal position. There was no denying it was me. He turned to me and straightened it out enough for me to read the caption. The caption on the photo read, **I've been sleeping with your wife.**

Sean began to speak. With every word his voice cracked.

"Minah, do you want to explain what the point in me busting my ass was? Making these deals and financially securing our future to reap a gun to my head and the deceit of the woman I loved indefinitely, as a reward! I did what I did for you!! And this is how you repay me?"

I began rambling and stuttering like a blithering idiot. How could I have been so stupid? And now I've risked my own husband's life.

"Oh my God baby, I'm sorry. I'm so so sorry, I was alone, you weren't home, I was just lonely Sean. Micah what the fuck are you doing?! How did you even know where I lived?! It was nothing baby I promise you, it was nothing. Please don't hurt him Micah. Please!" I cried.

"Shut up!" Micah shouted. "How does embarrassment feel Minah? Seeing your pictures on campus. You were so good to me baby, I wanted to share you with the world. I can't say the same for you. Every time we were together in public I had to act as if I was some distant relative, a stranger you just met right after I was in between your thighs!! Baby, I could kill him and we could be together, just like we always wanted."

"Micah those are things that you wanted" I said calmly as I moved towards him in hopes to retrieve the gun.

"Aminah, we were meant to be. Love knows no boundaries Aminah right? Just like in that Nirnatar poem." He said in desperation.

Micah began to recite from a poem I introduced the second week of class by Dr. Rajendra Tela Nirantar:

Love

Knows no boundaries

Is not limited to any

Age Cast color or creed

Comes naturally

In compassionate hearts

When two hearts vibe

With each other

Speak

The same language

Throb for each other

Comes instantly

Creates

An unending desire

Of being together

I recited along with him. By this time my husband was sweating profusely and I was near Micah enough to reach the gun and remove it from his grasp if I was quick enough. When we recited the last two lines in unison, I touched Micah's face. With a crazed glare he was tearful but firmly pressing the gun against my husband's temple. I've never seen anyone so broken other than the mirror image of the stranger that resembled myself. All I remembered at that point was my husband turning swiftly and the gun going off and my own screaming. This would be the last time I'd scream my lover's name.

Chapter 12

Aminah

I now realize that passion outside of a relationship is only ever going to be short lived, which in this case it was. Cheating is a selfish act. I will be the first to admit it. She could have chosen not to do what she did, but instead caused a chain reaction of pain. I realize that I wasn't happy with myself or in my marriage and willfully accepted another man's advances to close the gap and fulfill my needs. I should be able to express myself to the husband I love and at the very moment that I feel like he is unreachable I should do something other than engage in infidelity to get his attention. I believe that Aminah did really love her husband. I also believe Celeste and Laurisse relished that their friend wasn't so perfect after all but didn't expect anything quite like this to become of it. She mentioned she hadn't heard from either of them since she'd been serving time for Micah's murder. I couldn't imagine losing my friends, my career, my reputation, my livelihood.

I flashbacked to my final conversation with her.

"My husband pulled the trigger that night as he wrestled the gun from Micah's grasp. But I couldn't let him go to prison behind my actions." She said.

I truly understand her regret over what happened and I know that happiness is something that has got to come from within, first and foremost. It should not have been up to anyone else to compensate for what the men we are with won't do. After all, there is some reason we choose them to begin with. Micah was a prime example. He offered Aminah the 'Hero' fantasy. He did everything she wanted which allowed her to avoid any clear signs of danger. But how was she supposed to know that fool was crazy? Oh well that's no excuse. I too am pushing forty. My husband Kareem and I are successful. But our relationship is suffering and as a result I have sought the comfort of my lover. I don't know if I've stayed because I enjoy the idea of being married to my husband or if we need to go our separate ways and stop wasting each other's time. It isn't clear if he is physically cheating as well but it is crystal clear and quite evident that there was a problem in our marriage before I began my affair. I imagined marriage to be fun when we were in our twenties. Kareem and I were friends before marriage. Good friends. He was no stranger to me or my needs. We are both very ambitious people so I thought each day would be full of adventure, fresh ideas, and sex to celebrate our accomplishments. We would wake up in each other's arms and smile because he knew I had his back and he had mine. It's unfortunate that nights are cold. Distracted. And unsatisfying.

I drove home immediately after my move to appeal for lesser time in her conviction for the murder of Micah Ford. I also deleted my lovers' name from my phone and planned to change my phone number as soon as possible.

"Hey honey." I said as I walked through the door.

"Hey baby." My husband replied while lying on the couch. "How was court today?"

"It was interesting. Good though. I won my case."

"That's great love." He said while making absolutely no eye contact as he was texting away on his cell phone.

I snatched the phone out of his hand and threw it against the living room wall.

"Babe, what the hell was that about?"
"We need to talk." I said as I grabbed his hands. "I need to tell you something. But first I want to tell you about a woman named Aminah."

Teach Me

Teach me how to love because without your attention

I'm not sure

There are two men in my heart and I cannot find the cure

My husband's absence unexpectedly

is more than I can endure

Without getting my ways I appear immature

I've allowed another man in our bed

Communicated with him about my frustration instead

He ravished me in a way that made me reflect

my younger years

Stayed up late nights to gently dry my tears

He was a professor in his own right,

he knew just the right science

He commanded me when I wasn't in compliance

What I've lived is a lie, it's no love story

What do I say when I get caught? Poor me surely

And what about my lover, what does he get out of this?

A few stolen hours? Two tears and a kiss?

I've comprehended but I need you to instruct me dear

How do I get your attention? There's nothing I fear

Don't keep me a secret

I want you to say my name so loud the neighbors will speak it

Allow yourself to be my erotic muse

The only way to recollection is to infuse

I'll tease you at your request using only verbal intercourse

I want you as my only, I don't want a divorce

So let's pick up the pieces and see that they meet cohesively

I'll await for your instruction baby, just TEACH ME...

Author Bio

Courtney 'Phoenix' White is the author of the bestselling novel, 'Anybody's Somebody' as well as a plethora of published poems. The Author has a passion for teaching, writing, and photography. This fiery socialite is known primarily for Erotica however her genres have expanded over the years. She strives to be the voice of women who are afraid of expressing themselves not only sexually but assertively hence the moniker, Phoenix which represents rebirth and the ability to rise from the ashes vigor and new hope. Courtney 'Phoenix' White hails from Warren, Ohio where she was born and raised. Her literary journey began as she ventured into writing poetry during her high school years at Warren G. Harding. Courtney's debut title graced the world, Fall of 2013 via FreedomInk Publishing's urban imprint, Oppidian.

With the amazing support of fans, Phoenix has been featured in Pen'Ashe Magazine, on the cover of Conversations Magazine, interviewed on Conversations Live, toured in different cities for book signings and has received stellar 5 Star book reviews from reputable Readers.

There are some pretty amazing titles available at FreedomInk Publishing. You should totally check them out!

'Woman on Fire' by Trinette Collier

'Darkness Before the Dawn' by Dawn Miller

'Life & Love Through My Eyes'
by Ramona Jones

'The Loves Me Not' Trilogy by Kenny L. Mitchell

'Jareth, First Lord' by Mellie Miller

'Carnal Sobriety' by Katandra Shanel Jackson

An Urban Imprint of FreedomInk Publishing

www.freedomink365.com/oppidian

www.ingramcontent.com/pod-product-compliance
Lightning Source LLC
Chambersburg PA
CBHW030144200626
46812CB00015B/1452